STAY WITH YOU

Destiny Falls Prequel

ALEXA RIVERS

July - 12 Years Ago

Chapter One

KENNEDY

Snow everywhere. It had been snowing when I arrived in the small mountain village of Destiny Falls two days ago, but there was something different about seeing snow while tucked safely inside a well-heated cottage versus being out in it. The owner of the cottage I was renting had stocked a few essentials before I got to town, so I'd spent yesterday recovering from the flight to New Zealand from Los Angeles.

This was the first time I'd ventured from the cottage, and it was a shock to my system. Not only was it cold, but it was slippery. A born and bred Cali girl, I felt completely unprepared. I just hoped the ski resort where I'd been hired as a barista had good central heating.

I turned the Suzuki hatchback my stepfather had bought me as a "congratulations on beginning your grand adventure" gift onto a road with a sign pointing toward the ski resort and gritted my teeth. I'd chosen this car because it was similar to the one I'd had back home, and I figured it would be easier to drive on the wrong side of the road if I was at least comfortable in my vehicle, but I was starting to think that might have been a mistake. The small Suzuki didn't seem up to the task of navigating snow-covered roads. Perhaps I'd need to trade it in.

The road sloped steeply up ahead and veered around a tight bend. Slowing to a crawl, I swung around it and breathed a sigh of relief.

I shouldn't have.

The road twisted again, and this time, I wasn't ready for it.

My car hit the verge and the wheels skidded, trying to find a grip on a hidden patch of ice. The car tilted. My heart slammed into my chest.

Oh shit.

I was going over the edge.

The car rolled, and I screamed as it tumbled down the side of the hill. The world bounced crazily around me. Airbags burst from the front and sides, smashing into my face with bruising force. Black spots danced before my eyes. The seatbelt cut into my waist and shoulder as I fell forward. Hot liquid scalded my skin as coffee burst free of its carry cup.

Finally, the car juddered to a stop. Upside down.

I hung from the seat, blood rushing to my head. The engine was still running. If this were the movies, the car would burst into flames at any moment. My mind was fuzzy, my thoughts sluggish. I needed to cut the power. Hands shaking, I reached for the ignition, fumbling until I found the key and turned it. The engine died. At least that was one problem solved.

A ringing sound whined in my ears. I looked around but couldn't figure out what might be making it. Perhaps it was in my head. Trying to ignore it, I listened out for help, which would surely arrive soon, but then remembered I wasn't in L.A. anymore. I'd come off a snowy road in the middle of nowhere, and apart from the occasional sweep of headlights in the distance, I couldn't see any sign of human life. Who knew how long it might take for someone to realize I needed help, let alone for it to arrive?

My lower lip trembled. I was alone. Upside down. After my first traffic accident ever. My great adventure had gotten off to a terrible start. I stifled a sob. Damn it. I was supposed to be exploring exotic locations, putting my own wants first for once instead of always being the responsible oldest sibling, and discovering what I'd like to do with my future. Now I had to wonder if this was all a mistake. I wasn't equipped to be on my own. What the hell had I been thinking, announcing to my family that I was flying to the bottom of the world to "find myself"? How could I find myself when I wasn't even sure I could find my way out of this damned car?

I blinked rapidly to hold off the tears that threatened and tried to clear my head. The whining was fading away, but my thoughts were still slow.

Should I undo the seat belt? I didn't even know if I could with the way it was locked around my body, and if I did, I might injure myself if I landed in an awkward position when I fell. I reached for the roof. It wasn't that far beneath me, but even if I were to stick the landing, I wasn't sure I'd be able to get out because one side of the car seemed to be buried in a snowdrift.

I spotted my bag. It had fallen near where the roof met the windshield, but might be just within reach. Inside that bag was my phone. I stretched for it, coming up short on the first attempt, but when I strained against the seatbelt and bit my lip in concentration, I managed to brush the handle with my fingers. With another try, I gripped the edge of the fabric and eased it toward myself. When it was closer, I worked open the zipper and reached inside for my phone. Fortunately, the emergency number had been pre-programmed in, and I called it.

"You've reached emergency services," a brisk female voice said. "How can I direct your call?"

"I-I've been in a car accident," I stuttered. "My car is upside down in the snow. I need help."

"How many vehicles involved?"

"Just mine. I rolled off the road."

She made a thoughtful sound. "Are you injured? Is anyone with you?"

"I'm alone." Tears burned the backs of my eyes at the thought of how small that made me feel. As the oldest of five siblings, I wasn't used to being on my own, and as the daughter who usually took the safe option and made sure not to cause any fuss, I felt wholly unprepared. "I don't think I'm injured. At least, not seriously. A couple of bruises, and my head is shaken up."

"Can you get out?"

I glanced at the far door again. "Um, maybe."

"Is the engine off?"

"Yeah."

The sound of a keyboard clicking came over the line. "What's your location?"

I racked my brain. "I don't know the name of the road, but it's the one that goes up to Destiny Peak Ski Resort. I'm about half a mile past the turnoff."

"Okay, that's perfect." The woman's voice was calm and soothing. "Stay put and don't try to move. Help will be with you soon."

"Thank you." I ended the call and closed my eyes, realizing too late that I hadn't asked how long it would take.

It must have only been five or ten minutes later that I heard sirens, but it felt like forever. Lights flashed a short distance away, and then a face appeared by the window. A gorgeous, square-jawed face with messy blond hair sticking out from beneath a helmet.

"Hi." The man spoke loudly enough for me to hear

him through the window. He had dark blue eyes I could stare into forever. "I'm Liam. I'm here to get you out."

"Thanks." Suddenly, I wished my eyes and nose weren't red and puffy from a combination of the cold and finally having given in to the urge to cry.

"What's your name?" he asked as though we were standing in line for coffee and had all the time in the world.

"Kennedy," I told him. "Kennedy Carter."

He grinned. "Well, Kennedy Carter, today is your lucky day. You've got the best fire crew here to help you. You just follow my instructions, and we'll have you in a nice, toasty ambulance in no time."

My cheeks flushed with a combination of attraction and humiliation. I felt like melting at the sound of his sexy kiwi accent, but how embarrassing would it be to have an ambulance called? Nothing seemed to be broken or bleeding. "I don't need an ambulance."

His expression turned stern. "It's protocol for an accident like this. We need to make sure you're as fine as you seem."

I nodded. That made sense.

"Good. Now we're coming in for you. You ready?"

Chapter Two

LIAM

Wowzer.

Even when Kennedy Carter had been hanging upside down in her car, I could tell she was a looker, but now that she was right side up and sitting in the back of the ambulance while my best friend Asher checked her over, it was clear she was a knockout. Her hair was long, dark, and shiny. It looked like it would be soft to touch. And her eyes were incredible. A vivid shade of blue that made mine look dull by comparison. But it was the sweet way she smiled and the faint blush of her cheeks as she tried to assure everyone there was no need to worry that enchanted me.

As one of New Zealand's premier skiing destinations, Destiny Falls had a lot of international tourists visiting during winter. Some of them—especially the ones who stayed at the resort—seemed to think they were above the locals, but not this girl. She was obviously out of her depth driving a car that should never have been allowed on this road in snowy conditions, but she hadn't gotten defensive or aggressive like some visitors did when things went wrong. Instead, she'd seemed embarrassed by the whole situation. She sat quietly while Asher asked her questions and scanned her for potential injuries. Other than some deep bruising, she'd gotten lucky. Asher didn't seem to think she had a concussion, although he recommended she have someone nearby for the rest of the day to observe her.

Igor and Zane had retreated to the cab of the truck to keep warm. Only myself and Parks, who was in charge of our crew, remained near the ambulance to listen while Asher did his thing.

"So, where are you from?" Asher asked.

"Los Angeles." Her voice was soft, with a smooth American accent. "I only arrived a couple of days ago."

Parks made a sound of disapproval. "You should have had chains on your car—and a better-equipped vehicle. Make sure you buy chains before you head up the mountain again."

"Chains?" She cocked her head, clearly confused. "What for?"

"To keep you from sliding off the road," he said. "You should have done your research. I'd have thought anyone who bothered coming here to ski would at least be familiar with the safety tools needed."

"Oh." She looked chastened. "I'm sorry. I've made a mess of things." She met Parks's eyes, improving my opinion of her backbone. He could be an intimidating bastard.

His expression softened. "You did a good job turning off the engine and staying put though."

"Thanks. I didn't know about the chains. I'm not a tourist. I'm the new barista at the resort." Her face fell. "You don't think they'll fire me for being late on my first day, do you?"

"Of course not," I hurried to assure her, hoping it was true. "Have you spoken to them yet?"

"Oh my God." She slapped her palm to her forehead. "I can't believe I didn't think of that."

"You're still shaken." I wished I could hug her. She looked like she needed it. But she was in a foreign country, and I doubted she wanted a random man putting his hands on her. "You're bound to forget things. But letting them know soon will probably go a long way to help the situation."

She nodded miserably and mumbled something.

"Okay, I think you're fine," Asher announced, stepping back. "But you should rest today and make sure someone checks on you every couple of hours. You won't be up to starting a new job. You need time to recover."

Her shoulders slumped. "Ugh. Just perfect."

"You can ride back into town with me," he said. "You'll have to get your car towed, and it will need some repairs."

She looked from him to me and asked quietly, "How do I do that?"

Parks sighed as though she was a lost cause.

"We'll get you sorted," I promised. "Call D.F. Motors and ask for Jimmy. Explain what happened, and he'll get your car and sort out anything else you need."

A flicker of relief crossed her face. "D.F. Motors," she repeated. "Jimmy. Thanks, Liam. That really helps."

Her praised warmed me, and I shrugged it away. "It's a small town. Everyone knows everyone, and we help out where we can. Let's get you home."

We piled into the vehicles and made the journey back to the station, which was located on a road off Centennial Street, the main commercial street of Destiny Falls township. The ambulance didn't join us, so I assumed Asher was taking Kennedy directly to wherever she was staying.

I swallowed disappointment at the thought of not seeing her again, but then remembered she had a job at the resort, so she was presumably going to be around for a while. She might need new friends too. Friends, I could do. More than that wouldn't be such a great idea. Not so soon after Zoe dumped me, and especially not with someone from L.A. If I couldn't even stomach the idea of moving somewhere else in New Zealand, it would be stupid to get attached to someone from halfway around the world who lived in a dirty, giant city that represented everything I hated. Urban jungles and wannabe celebrities weren't my thing.

We parked and got out.

"Coffee, anyone?" Igor asked, already on his way to the staff room.

"Yeah," I called after him. A hot drink would warm my fingers nicely, even if the crap we kept around here barely passed for real coffee. I headed after him, and Zane followed. Parks went to his office.

By the time Asher returned, we were seated around a table, playing cards. He grabbed his mug, which Igor had filled and set on the counter, and pulled up a chair.

"So, what'd you think of her?" Asher asked, his tone teasing.

I rolled my eyes. Ever since Zoe had blown out of town without giving me the slightest bit of warning, Asher had been on at me to hook up with someone else, so I knew exactly where this was going.

"She's pretty," I admitted.

"She's beautiful," he countered. "And a little shy. I know how you like them that way."

I pulled a face. I couldn't help it. Women who blushed easily endeared themselves to me. "I'm not looking for anything," I reminded him. "Especially not with an American who'll eventually be going back to where she came from."

Asher shrugged. "You don't have to marry her. Just ask her out. Buy her a drink. See how it goes."

"Nope." I played a card and looked at Igor and Zane for support. "You get it, right? A girl like that, she's not going to stay in Destiny Falls for long. She'll be back in L.A. in no time, and I couldn't be happy anywhere but here. This place is in my blood."

Asher groaned and buried his face in his palms. "What part of 'you don't have to marry her' don't you understand? She doesn't have to be your happily ever after. She can be a pleasant stop-off along the way."

"He has a point," Zane offered.

I shot him a look. "You know me. I can't do casual. I get attached, and then it ends badly because, apparently, no one other than me wants to live in a tiny town in the mountains." I deflated. "Not even for love."

I would never move away from Destiny Falls. Every quaint street and old-fashioned building was carved onto my heart. My family was here, and my friends. Any time I left, even for a road trip or vacation, I missed the fresh, clean scent of the air, the glorious green surroundings, and the biting cold of winter and dry heat of summer.

I supposed my refusal to even consider moving elsewhere was why Zoe had abandoned me. Months later, her defection still hurt. We'd been dating for two years, and I'd thought she wanted the same things as me. Then, back in January, I'd dropped by her parents' place to visit and discovered she'd left for university in Auckland the day before. She'd left a goddamned Dear John letter to break up with me and hadn't had the guts to deliver it herself.

She claimed she'd been hinting that she wanted to leave for months, but I either hadn't picked up on it or hadn't cared enough to do anything about it. In hindsight, I could see the signs, but I'd been oblivious at the time. In the end, she said, she'd decided she couldn't be stuck in a go-nowhere place forever, so she'd just gone.

This girl, Kennedy, with her sexy accent and incredible eyes, would do the same.

"I'm on Team Liam here," Igor said in his thick French accent. "You've got to play to your strengths."

Asher sighed. "Just promise me you'll think about it."

"Fine," I relented. "I'll think about it, but that's it."

He grinned. "Good. Can you deal me in?"

Chapter Three

KENNEDY

The next day, I was eating breakfast in my cozy cottage, wondering exactly how I was going to get myself up to the ski resort, when there was a sharp knock on the door. I answered it to find a red-faced man in his fifties wearing a grease-streaked sweater.

"You Kennedy?" he asked.

"Yes."

He stuck out a hand. "I'm Jimmy. I've got your car on the road."

"Is it drivable?" I'd already spoken yesterday to the insurance company my stepfather, Malcolm, used, and I ordered a more suitable vehicle to be delivered later in the week. Perks of having a mother who married into a rich family. I might not always get much in the way of attention —it was difficult for Mom and Malcolm to focus on me when they had my much younger siblings to deal with— but I never wanted for material things.

"It's in pretty good shape, considering," he said. "I've replaced the window and the front bumper, buffed out a couple of dents, and put a set of chains in the trunk. The hood is a bit crumpled. Completely safe, but not a great look. I can order a replacement if you need. I didn't have anything suitable at the workshop."

"Thanks so much." It was a relief to know I'd be able to get to work without having to wait for my new car to arrive. "Don't worry about the hood for now. I'll let you know if I need one." But I'd probably just sell the car as it was once the new one arrived. "How much do I owe you?"

He lifted one shoulder and let it drop. "The bill is on the passenger seat, but no hurry. I'm sure you've got more important things to sort out right now."

I sighed. Yeah, I still hadn't made up my mind about how I'd be getting to the resort today. Theoretically, the car solved that, but after being stuck upside down yesterday, waiting for help to come, the idea of driving didn't appeal to me.

"Thanks. Is there a local taxi service?"

He raised a brow. "Liam didn't tell you?"

"Tell me what?" I was confused. What did Liam, the gorgeous firefighter, have to do with anything?

"We talked this morning. I'm going to run you up to the resort, and he'll pick you up at the end of his shift." He tipped his head toward her. "Today only, mind you."

"There's really no need for that." It was a kind gesture, but I didn't want to take up any more of his or Liam's time than I already had. Even if it made my stomach flutter to think that Liam wanted to help me. "I'd hate to put you out."

Jimmy looked like he was fighting a smile. "Look, kid. You're new around here, so you don't know how things work yet. We take care of our own. We help each other. Besides"—the grin finally spread across his face—"I'm the closest you'll find to a taxi in these parts, so unless you want to wait for one to drive up from Queenstown, you'll have to make do."

"Oh." Well, there wasn't much I could say to that. "Okay then. Thank you."

"No problem." He nodded to the door. "Mind if I come in while you get your bag? I'm freezing my ass off."

"Of course."

I stepped aside to let him in, wondering briefly if it was a good idea to let a strange man into my home, but concern about missing another day of work outweighed that worry. My new boss, Tabitha, had been very understanding when I spoke to her yesterday, but I didn't want to push my luck. I cleaned up the breakfast dishes and went to the bedroom to get my bag.

The bedroom had white walls and pale pink curtains, the same as the rest of the cottage. The decor was feminine but not over-the-top. A bathroom came off the hall, and the living area and kitchen were joined in an open-plan setup. The cottage was different from the large home in L.A. where I'd spent the past few years of my life, but I liked it. The landlady, Grace, seemed nice too. She wasn't much older than me, but she had a sense of self-assurance I lacked.

"I'm ready," I told Jimmy.

"Let's hit the road, then. The sooner we're there, the sooner I can get back to the workshop."

We drove to the ski resort in Jimmy's tow truck. He took the journey slow and shared plenty of advice about how to avoid getting into trouble again. Despite his rough edges, he seemed thoughtful. He bid me goodbye when we arrived, and I got out. As I turned away and looked up at the resort, my jaw dropped. It was like something out of a fairytale, comprising several buildings with brick exteriors and massive windows overlooking the snow-covered hills. A balcony curled around the main building. With light glowing from within and snow thick on the roof, it reminded me, oddly, of a gingerbread house.

Skiers dotted the slopes, but I would rather curl up in the warmth with a book and a mug of hot chocolate than join them. I smiled to myself. Perhaps my year of adventure was looking up.

MY FIRST DAY OF WORK WAS A SUCCESS. HOWEVER MUCH of a disaster I might be outside the resort, I could deliver a good cup of coffee, thanks to a childhood spent in my parent's coffee shop.

Tabitha, my boss, was lovely. She'd welcomed me with a smile and set me to work, pairing me with another barista for support. At the end of the day, I was tired of being on my feet, but my insides were warm with the satisfaction that came from a job well done. I knew I was going to fit in here just fine.

"You look happy."

I jumped in surprise at the masculine voice and spun around to see Liam standing near the entrance. He raised a hand and smiled.

"I am happy," I told him. "Today was much better than yesterday. Hang on a sec." I told my colleague I was heading off and checked to make sure I had everything I'd brought with me. "Thanks for organizing a ride. You didn't have to do that."

His eyes flicked up and met mine, and he smiled. "I wanted to." He winked. "I'd like to get to know you better, so this is totally selfish."

I shook my head. Somehow, I doubted he was selfish. He seemed like a good guy, through and through. "Thanks."

"This way." He strode outside. I followed him to a dirty Ute that was well-kept but had seen better days. He unlocked it, and I got into the passenger seat and buckled up. When he started the engine, the heater purred to life. I thrust my hands in front of it, eager to defrost my fingers.

"I'm not used to the temperature here," I confessed. "I knew it would be chilly, but I underestimated just how cold it could get."

He nodded. "Fair enough. It's a pretty big change from Los Angeles."

"It sure is." I glanced at him as he steered us through the parking lot and onto the road. "Have you ever been?"

He looked surprised. "To L.A.? No, and I have no desire to. Traffic, smog, people everywhere, and cityscape as far as the eye can see." He shuddered. "Sounds like my kind of hell. Not to mention how far it is from my family, and the fact that, from what I can tell, half the people there are phony and self-obsessed." He shook his head. "I don't want to be anywhere but here." He shot me a look, his eyes unreadable. "I grew up in Destiny Falls, and I'll be happy if I never leave."

I pursed my lips, wondering whether to be offended by his obvious disdain for my hometown, but from his tone, I imagined he'd say much the same thing about any place that wasn't Destiny Falls. I was actually a little envious.

"That must be nice." I wished I was so certain of my place in the world. I'd always been restless, and had the sense that I wasn't where I was supposed to be, but hadn't known how to change that.

"Yeah. It is." He took a turn with more speed than I expected, and I flinched, but we rounded it smoothly. "So, why did you fly all the way from L.A. to New Zealand to work at a resort in a tiny town in the mountains?"

I felt a telltale prickle that probably meant I was blushing. Thanks to my fair skin, it happened easily. "I've always wanted to see New Zealand, and I didn't know what to do after I graduated high school, so I decided to take a year off from making any major decisions. I chose Destiny Falls because it had an opening for a barista and looked about as different from home as possible. I wanted a change." My cheeks heated further. "But, as has been pointed out, I didn't come very prepared."

He smiled sympathetically. "You'll get there. For what it's worth, I think it's brave as hell to get a job on the other side of the world and just go for it. Not many people would do that."

I laughed. "I don't feel brave."

Maybe I had when I arrived at the airport and collected my luggage, but no longer. I'd been sure that getting some space from my parents and siblings—much as I loved them—would help me gain some perspective on the future. I had a few career ideas, but I'd had it drummed into me over the years that I needed to make responsible decisions. While that approach might have helped me get good grades and be a positive role model for my little sister and brothers, it had gotten to the point where I was out of touch with what I actually wanted.

"Have you made any friends yet?" he asked.

"I've hardly met anyone." I thought on it. "Grace, who's renting the cottage to me, seems nice. So do the people at the resort. And you. But I haven't actually made any plans with anyone."

"Grace is great. She's my brother Nate's best friend."

I should have realized he'd know her. It seemed like the kind of town where everyone knew everyone.

"What are you doing this weekend?" he asked.

Flutters erupted in my stomach. I pressed my palms to my jeans and, with an effort, managed not to stare at him. "No plans."

"You do now," he told me. "I'm taking you skiing." He looked across the car. "If you'd like to, of course. No pressure."

"I would." The words were out of my mouth before I

had time to think them through. Then, when I did, I panicked, wanting to take them back. I couldn't ski. I'd never skied before in my life. I'd only seen snow once before I arrived in New Zealand.

"Perfect." He sent me a smile, his eyes crinkling at the edges. "Can I pick you up at eight on Saturday morning? It's best to get there early to beat the rush."

Ugh. I bit my tongue. Should I tell him? Getting invited out with him was more than I'd hoped for, and I didn't want to make a fuss when he was trying to be nice. Perhaps I could just figure it out as we went along. I'd watch a few instructional videos ahead of time. It couldn't be that hard, and I could hardly say no to a gorgeous fire-fighter who'd pulled me out of an upturned car. Strip off a couple of layers of clothes, give him a puppy, and he would pretty much qualify for Mr. January in a smutty charity calendar.

"It's a plan. I'll give you my number in case you need to get in touch."

I really hoped he would.

Chapter Four

LIAM

When I arrived to pick up Kennedy on Saturday morning, my stomach was a riot of nerves. She looked adorable bundled up in cold weather gear, her face peeking out from above a multi-colored knitted scarf that looked like one of the ones Grace's aunt Desdemona sold at her shop on Centennial Street. I wondered if Kennedy had done some research after her accident on Monday to make sure she wasn't caught unprepared again. Perhaps it was strange, but I liked the idea of that.

"Hey, you." I greeted her with a smile and waited while she locked up, then led her to my Ute. My skiing gear was in the back, and I'd borrowed my younger brother, Toby's, equipment for her since when I'd messaged her earlier, she'd said she didn't own any herself, and they were a similar size. If they didn't fit, we could always rent what we needed instead.

I asked her about her week and listened to the highlights of her new job while I drove to the turnoff. We cruised for a while until we drew near the resort and encountered traffic. I slowed and followed behind. When we arrived, I got out and went around to the trunk get our stuff out.

"Do you have anything you need to put in a locker?" I asked.

"I don't think so." She slipped her wallet into her pocket and grabbed a pair of gloves from the car.

"Cool. Wait here while I go get us a day pass, and then we can head for the beginner slopes." I quirked a brow. "Unless you want to start somewhere else?"

"Nope." She popped the "p." "Beginner slopes sound good to me." She touched my arm. "But I can pay my share."

"It's my treat. You haven't been paid by the resort yet, have you?" I shouldn't do things that make our outing seem more datelike, but I couldn't seem to help myself. At first, I'd planned to invite a couple of friends, or perhaps some of my siblings—I had five to choose from—to join us, but I hadn't been able to bring myself to do it. Stupid or not, I wanted to spend time with her, and I wanted to do it alone. Perhaps Asher was right, and I should just bite the bullet, ask her out, and then deal with the consequences when she inevitably returned to Los Angeles.

"No, but I can afford it," she replied.

"I'd like to do this for you," I said. "Consider it a gesture of friendship."

Yeah, sure. Friendship. That's why I dreamed of her naked last night.

I left before she could argue and hurried into the small shop attached to the resort, where they dealt with ski passes and equipment rentals. At the counter, I asked for two day passes and pocketed them before heading back out into the cold. Kennedy was waiting where I'd left her, cheeks pink from the cool wind, lips pursed and looking 100 percent kissable. My heart gave a *ka-thunk* when she raised her eyes and smiled.

"Thanks," she said.

"You're welcome." I shouldered as much of the gear as I could and waited for her to take the rest. "This way." I led her toward a bench beside a gentle slope on the edge of the parking lot where a few children and their harried-looking parents were gliding—or stumbling—over the snow. "So, tell me about your family."

She watched as I sat on the bench and started pulling my gear on, then did the same. "I have four younger siblings." She snuck a look at me, her forehead scrunched as though she was trying to figure out what I was doing. "One full and three half."

"Do you need a hand?" I asked as she tugged at her laces.

"I've got it." She gave me an unconvincing smile. "My brother, Blair, is in high school. He's the only other kid from Mom's first marriage." A flicker of pain passed over her features. "My dad died when I was young."

"I'm sorry." I felt a pang. I loved my parents to bits. I couldn't imagine losing one of them.

She blew out a breath. "Yeah, it sucked. I miss him. But Mom's new husband, Malcolm, is awesome, and so are my half sister and brothers, Mina, Jamie, and Joel."

"Are they much younger than you?" I finished with my shoes and watched her out the corner of my eye. I'd known it was unlikely Kennedy had skied much before, but I was beginning to wonder if she'd done it at all. I itched to help her, but she'd said she didn't want it and until she indicated otherwise, I needed to respect that.

"Mina is nine, and the twins are eight." She finished her shoes and wobbled to her feet.

"I have twin siblings too," I told her. "Nate and Max are twenty-two. Nate is at police college and Max is studying to be a doctor."

"Wow." Her eyes widened. "Your family likes to help people, huh?"

I shrugged, uncomfortable with the praise. Perhaps that was the case for Max who had the biggest heart of anyone I knew, but for Nate and I, it was more a matter of wanting a job we could do locally and that wouldn't bore us out of our minds. "They're not the only twins. Summer and Toby, the youngest, are still in school."

"Two sets of twins?" She sounded stunned. "Your poor parents."

I chuckled. "Yeah. It can't have been easy, but we seem to have turned out all right."

We finished getting ready and made our way onto the slope.

"So, there are five kids in your family?" she asked. "Same as me?"

"Six," I corrected. "Nate and Max are the oldest, then there's me. My brother, Connor, is between me and the younger twins. He's at school too, although not for much longer."

"Do you like being part of such a big family?"

I grinned. "I love it. They're crazy, but that's part of the fun. One day, I want heaps of kids of my own. At least four."

"Really?" She stared at me, apparently dumbstruck, but then a smile broke over her face. "Me too! I love the idea of having a big family, but it's rare to find anyone else our age who agrees."

We shared a moment of mutual appreciation. Her smile lit her features, and it would be so easy to lean over and kiss the tip of her nose, but I resisted.

Friends, I reminded myself.

Somehow, I had a feeling I was fighting a losing battle. But if Kennedy was as perfect as I was beginning to think she was, then maybe I'd be happy to lose.

"Should we start over here?" I asked.

She nodded and thrust her chin forward in determination. "I'm ready."

"You're sure?"

She nodded again, but I wasn't so certain. At least on a gentle slope like this, she should be safe if anything was to go wrong. I set off and waited for her to join me. She was unsteady but kept her balance well, so I relaxed. Perhaps I'd been mistaken about her level of experience. But then we reached the bottom, and she showed no signs of slowing.

"How do I stop?" she cried out, already far enough ahead of me that I couldn't reach out to help her. She tumbled to her knees inches before hitting the railing at the end of the slope.

I rushed over to her. "Are you okay?"

She groaned and clambered awkwardly to her feet, testing each leg. "I'm fine." She winced. "It's mostly my pride that's bruised."

"Thank God for that." I checked her over and agreed that she looked all right. "Form a pizza slice with your skis. That's how you stop."

Her blush deepened. "I should have known that. I guess this is the part where I admit I've never been skiing before."

Yup. Called it.

"Why didn't you tell me?"

"I'm sorry, I know I should have." She brushed snow off her sleeve with her other hand instead of meeting my eyes. "It's just… Well… it was really nice of you to invite me, and I didn't want to be a nuisance. Plus, I get the impression you can do basically anything, and I feel like a bumbling city girl by comparison."

She was sweet, but misguided. I moved forward and clasped her gloved hands. "I'm flattered, but you don't have to pretend to be someone you're not. I don't mind teaching you. I'd rather you were straight with me."

"Okay." She pursed her lips, her expression guilty. "I'm sorry." She pulled one of her hands away and waved as if we were meeting for the first time. "Hi. I'm Kennedy Carter, hopeless city girl. I've never skied, and until this week, I didn't know that chains existed other than in the context of jewelry or prison. I'm completely out of my element."

I shook my head, amused despite myself. "Hi, Kennedy. I'm Liam. I'd love to be your guide to Destiny Falls and your teacher on the slopes. Especially if you let me show off my knowledge and maybe steal a kiss or two along the way."

She smiled shyly. "If you play your cards right."

Screw friendship.

I leaned over and pressed my lips to hers. The kiss was chaste and sweet, but attraction zinged through my body, and the hairs on my arms stood up. Our connection was electric. I could only imagine how it would be if we were somewhere private. But there was no hurry. I wanted to savor this. My mouth curved against hers. Provided she felt the same, this would be the first kiss of many.

October

Chapter Five

KENNEDY

I scanned the items arrayed on the cottage floor one last time. "You're sure that's everything?"

"We're fully covered," Liam replied. "Food, clothes, emergency supplies. We've got enough to stay away for another day or two if anything goes wrong."

Nerves blasted through me. After spending the past couple of months in Destiny Falls, I knew just how badly things could go wrong for hikers on the trails near the township. It seemed like a search-and-rescue expedition had to be mounted at least once every couple of weeks. Liam and I had been on day hikes before but not an overnighter. This would actually be the first night we'd spent together at all. Another thing to worry about. I'd never slept with a guy before. I knew Mom had been concerned about me making bad decisions with sex, so I'd just never gone there. Now, I was ready, but still nervous about taking the leap.

"Not that it will," he added, catching sight of my expression and misreading it. "The weather forecast is good, it's sunny, we're both fit and healthy. Not to mention that you've got a local guide on your side." He winked. "Relax, Kenz. We're going to have a great time."

At that, I smiled. "I know." I just couldn't help being a little anxious. This was so far outside my comfort zone. But then, the past few weeks with Liam had been all about exploring new territory together and doing things because I wanted to rather than because they were the so-called "responsible" option. "Should we pack everything?"

"Yes. Just remember what I said."

"Less squishable things at the bottom," I chorused, having heard it a dozen times already. "Emergency supplies near the top."

"Good." He flashed a grin that made me melt inside. Even after our short time together, I knew Liam was different from any boys I'd dated before. He made me think about things like forever. I loved his family, too. They were warm, welcoming, and slightly chaotic, much like my own.

We finished packing and shouldered our bags. Mine was heavy, but not so much that I couldn't walk with it. We carried them to his Ute and put them in the back, then I dashed to the cottage to check we hadn't left anything behind. I locked up and returned.

I had a Subaru now, which was more suited to the roads around here, but we'd decided to take Liam's vehicle since he knew the way and I still had a hard time driving on the left side of the road if I detoured from my usual routes.

I tuned into a local radio station, and we sang along to Lorde and Six60 as we drove out of town toward a walking trail that led up the Castle River Valley, which was apparently less traveled than the more popular track to Destiny Falls or Destiny Tarn.

Liam turned onto a gravel road and slowed as we bumped over several potholes. We followed the road until it ended at a small grass clearing. A green sign with yellow writing indicated where the trail began. I swallowed, nerves crowding my stomach. Liam had said earlier that I was fit, but I didn't feel it—especially when I knew we'd be hiking several hundred vertical feet.

Forest surrounded the clearing, but from the photos Liam had shown me, I knew that by the time we reached the hut, we'd be in open tussock land. I hadn't fully appreciated the amount of effort that might involve until now.

I slid from the car and straightened my back, determined not to be cowed. This was my year of adventure, and it was all about figuring out my limits and where I wanted my life to go. This was an important stepping stone. Besides, I trusted Liam not to drag me into something I wasn't prepared for. I rounded the front of the car and planted a kiss on his lips.

He chuckled. "What's that for?"

I shrugged. "Just felt like it."

He wrapped his arms around me, resting his hands on my lower back, and returned the kiss. My lips parted, and it grew heated. Liam groaned. "None of that, or we'll never get anywhere."

I sighed, knowing he was right. Though we hadn't had sex yet, our make-out sessions were growing hotter and heavier every time. I yearned for him to be inside me, but I worried he'd find me lacking. He'd never said so, but I was ninety percent sure he'd been intimate with his ex. Once again, he had experience I didn't.

"Fine." Pouting, I broke away and got my pack from the car. With a grunt of effort, I pulled it on, and then clipped the waistband shut and cinched it tight.

Liam did the same with his, then fussed with my straps, changing the length until they met with his satisfaction. When he was done, he placed his hands on my shoulders and looked into my eyes. "You got this."

I nodded, the certainty in his deep blue gaze instilling me with a sense of confidence. "Let's do it."

He led the way to the trail. It was only wide enough to walk in single file, and he glanced over his shoulder as we entered the shelter of the trees. I shot him a reassuring smile, then looked around, my eyes widening as I noted the way the sun filtered through the forest, casting golden patches of light and shadows. My fingers twitched, itching to get out the camera I'd slotted into the front pocket of my pack. I loved taking photographs, and I'd been capturing them nonstop since I arrived in Destiny Falls. Several of the ones I'd taken from the ski resort had come out so well that I was considering asking Tabitha whether she'd be open to selling them as postcards at the shop in the resort. I hadn't worked up the courage yet though. I was handy with a camera but hardly a professional.

For the first half hour, the trail wound peacefully through the forest on a reasonably level path, meandering around bends in the river and skirting larger trees. Liam stopped every so often to make sure I was keeping up and enjoying myself. But when the trail sloped upward, I started to struggle. My thighs burned with every step, and my breath came in gasps.

"You okay?" Liam called as he paused at a curve in the trail a few feet above me.

I wiped my sweaty face on my shirt and tromped upward. "I'm." *Pant.* "Doing." *Gasp.* "Fine."

His lips twitched, and I glared, silently daring him to comment. "Good news. There's a lookout up ahead with a bench where we can sit down for a few minutes."

"Thank God." I placed a foot on a tree root that formed a makeshift stair and grunted as I pushed up. "Dying."

He pressed his lips together to hide a smile. "I thought you were fine?"

I scoffed, pausing with a hand to my chest. "I lied."

I counted another fifty steps before Liam and I arrived at a raised platform that looked out over the surrounding forest. I raised a hand to my eyes to shield them from the sun, which was brighter here, and took in the view. Breathtaking. Thousands of treetops stretched into the horizon, bisected by a narrow blue-green line that must be Castle River. We'd veered away from the water earlier, but Liam said we'd rejoin it.

"Drink?" Liam asked, offering me a bottle.

I grabbed it from him and drank, grateful for the coolness on my parched throat. "Thanks." I unloaded my backpack and took my camera from the front pocket, then snapped a few photographs of the view. "I want one of you too," I told him, gesturing for him to stand in front of the lookout.

He complied with a good-natured smile, having been the subject of many of my pictures since we'd met. I loved capturing the moments in time we shared. Especially ones like this when it was just the two of us with no one else around for miles. He looked so handsome with flushed cheeks and sparkling eyes. The muscles of his arms bulged as he tucked his thumbs beneath the straps of his pack, and I shifted from one leg to the other, warding off a poorly-timed bolt of lust.

"There." I checked the last picture I'd taken to stop myself from ogling him. "All done."

"Nuh-uh." Liam grabbed my hand and tugged me closer, brushing a kiss over my mouth. "Now we're done."

Chapter Six

LIAM

Even flushed and tired from a long day of hiking, Kennedy was the most beautiful woman I'd ever seen. She looked up from her camera that was sitting on her lap as she scanned through the photographs she'd taken earlier, and she smiled. Something fluttered in my chest. Realizing I was staring, I bent to add a piece of wood to the old-fashioned fireplace. It could get cold out here, and I didn't want her first memory of spending the night with me to be tainted by something preventable, so I was keeping it nice and toasty.

The hut was rustic, with a stainless steel counter running along the length of one wall, three sets of bunk beds along another two walls, and the fireplace in the center of the room. A wooden table sat in front of the only window which overlooked a tussocked area that had been golden in the dying light of day but was now mostly hidden from view. Even inside, we could hear the gurgle of the Castle River, although it was at least a hundred meters away.

When we'd arrived earlier, we'd used the river to clean

off the worst of the sweat and changed into fresh clothes. I wasn't accustomed to seeing Kennedy in merino tights and a thermal singlet, but she looked adorable. Shadows played across her face from the light cast by the candles. We'd eaten a dinner of freeze-dried pasta and powdered soup, and the sky had darkened outside. I'd been keeping an eye out for any hikers who might arrive later in the evening, but at this point, it was reasonably safe to say we were alone for the night.

I prowled to the low bunk bed Kennedy was sitting on and sprawled along the mattress, wriggling until my head was on her lap.

She glanced down at me. "Is this your subtle way of saying you want my attention?"

"Subtlety is overrated."

She switched her camera off and set it aside, then sifted her fingers through my hair. I leaned into the touch, loving the way her fingertips felt against my scalp.

"I've had a really nice day." Her voice was soft and warm. "Thanks for bringing me here. It's a special place."

My heart jumped happily. "I'm glad you like it."

Zoe had never been much for the outdoors. Perhaps that should have been a warning that she wouldn't be happy in Destiny Falls long term, but I'd dismissed it.

Kennedy made a contented sound that zapped straight to my cock. I shut my eyes and tried to think of rock climbing, which was completely unsexy, to bring my thickening erection under control.

"I like Destiny Falls," she continued, the repetitive motion of her fingers through my hair, calming me. "I've always felt like I was missing something, but I didn't know what." Her thumbs paused at my temples and began to massage them. "Here, I don't feel that." I could hear the smile in her voice and opened my eyes so I could see the beautiful curve of those plump pink lips. "I'm beginning to think that maybe I've found the place I'm meant to be."

Bubbles of joy fizzed inside me, and I found myself holding my breath. Did she mean what I thought she did? Was she saying that she might want to stay here even after her gap year was over? I bit my lip. It was too much to hope for, but I desperately wanted it to be true. I hated the idea of saying goodbye to her at the end of the year, even though I knew I couldn't follow her back to L.A. City living wasn't for me—and L.A. was a city that represented the worst of everything. Was there a chance I could have the best of both worlds?

"Yeah?" I asked, aiming for nonchalance and failing.

"Yeah."

She eased my head off her lap and lay down so we were side by side with her facing me. She looked apprehensive but determined. I turned gooey inside.

"What do you think of that?" she asked.

I wrapped an arm around her and kissed the top of her head. "I think that would be amazing." I took a deep breath, knowing I needed to tell her exactly what had happened with Zoe, so she'd understand why this was such a big deal to me. "You know how I mentioned my ex?"

She stiffened. "The one who left?" Her tone was wary.

"I never realized she wanted out of Destiny Falls," I admitted. "It completely blindsided me when she was just gone one day."

"Wait." She raised herself up on her elbow. "She didn't say anything first? She just left?"

"Yep."

Her eyes narrowed and flashed dangerously. "That's awful! You must have been devastated."

I did a weird half-shrug thing because yeah, at the time, I'd been pretty broken up, but now that I had Kennedy, I didn't feel so raw from Zoe leaving, and I didn't want to give her any reason to doubt my feelings for her. "Anyway, it means a lot to hear you say you think you might have found your place because I've been so worried you might take off like she did and decide you don't see a future here. Since *my* future is here, that would mean we couldn't be together, and I'd miss you so badly."

Kennedy dipped her head to kiss me, her eyelashes fluttering as her eyes closed. Her breath whispered against my skin. "I see my future with you. If that doesn't, you know, scare you away. Otherwise, I can totally play it cool."

I erased the distance between us once, twice, then again. She tasted intoxicating. Like the forest, with a hint of mint from her toothpaste, and a sweetness underlying it that was all Kennedy. "What scares me is the thought of you leaving."

"You don't need to worry about that."

My heart felt like a mug that had been filled too full, with liquid oozing over the brim. I wanted to believe her. I just hoped she didn't change her mind. After all, we hadn't been together for very long.

"Like I've told you before," I added. "I'm a Destiny Falls lifer. This place is my home. But it would make me really happy if it could be your home too."

She smiled. "I'd like that." She hesitated for a moment, then sighed. "Just so you know, I'm, um." Her breath stuttered. "I'm a virgin."

I nuzzled her, rubbing my nose against hers. "I know."

"I don't want to be anymore." The words came out in a rush, and I pulled back to look at her face. Her expression was sleepy and desirous, with just a trace of worry—as if there was any chance I might say no to her.

"I wish I could give you my virginity too." I felt a pang at the thought. I'd never regretted having sex with Zoe until I met Kennedy. Now, I wished I could take back all of my firsts and give them to her.

"Hey." Her brow furrowed. "No regrets, okay? There's nothing for you to feel guilty about. The fact you have some idea what you're doing isn't a bad thing."

I kissed her forehead and watched the grooves ease. "Don't be worried. I would never do anything to hurt you."

Her smile made me wish I could pull the moon from the sky outside and hand it to her. "I trust you."

It wasn't "I love you", but it was damn close.

Chapter Seven

KENNEDY

Liam rolled on top of me, cradling me between his powerful thighs. The look in his eyes changed from affectionate to intense. He kissed me, and I parted my lips and met his tongue with mine. They slid against each other, and he rocked against the juncture of my thighs, his hard-on stealing my breath away. We'd made out plenty before, but never when I knew exactly where I wanted it to end: with us naked and writhing together.

I pressed up, deepening the friction between us, and he groaned. I skimmed my fingers along the gap between the fabric of his T-shirt and his track pants, enjoying the texture of his happy trail against my skin and the heat radiating from his body. My caresses traveled north, traversing the ridges of his abdomen, which was firm from spending time at the fire station gym between callouts. As my hands moved, his shirt edged up, revealing more of his torso and chest. It was pale—probably because we'd only recently come out of winter—and when I toyed with his nipple, it tightened to a nub. He knelt upright for long enough to yank his shirt over his head and cast it aside.

I stared at his chest, his pecs, and the delicious fuzz arrowing down to the waistband of his pants. I pushed at Liam's chest and he let me guide him onto his back. We had to be careful, maneuvering the two of us on a single bunk bed, but as long as we were cautious, it would be fine. I traced the curves and dips of his body, exploring them by touch, learning where he was sensitive or ticklish. When I dragged my fingernails lightly down his stomach, he groaned, and the tent behind his pants flexed.

I tentatively trailed a hand down to cup the bulge. "Can I?"

He gave a strained laugh. "Whatever you want."

My lips curved in a feline smile. Perhaps I didn't have much hands-on experience, but I could tell he was enjoying this. I slipped my hand under the waistband. My eyes widened as it encountered silky skin covering hard flesh.

"Didn't see much point wearing underwear when it's only us here," he explained.

My fingers reflexively curled around him and pumped. His hips jerked.

"A bit tighter," he said, gasping when I did as he said. His head fell back but he didn't take his eyes off me. "You're amazing, Kenz."

I wrapped my fist around the head of his cock, slicking through precum, and lowered my head to kiss him. He kissed me back, losing some of his usual finesse. It was wild. Messy. And it made fire pulse in my veins.

Suddenly, Liam was pushing me back, flipping me over, moving down my body, pausing at the hem of my tights as though to ask permission.

"Do it," I urged, lifting my hips to help him get them off while I wrestled out of my long-sleeved singlet, which left me in only my bra and panties. They were plain and conventional, since I'd known that if it came to it, I might have to hike in them, and practicality trumped sensuality, at least in this case. I started to remove my bra, but Liam stopped me with a hand over mine.

"Let me," he growled. Gently, he reached behind me and undid the clasp. His breath caught and he looked at my breasts almost reverently, then raised his eyes to mine. "You're perfect."

My throat tightened with emotion, so I just nodded. He seemed to understand. A smile softened his expression and he brushed a kiss over my lips before lowering his face to tease first one nipple and then the other with his mouth, lips, and tongue. The faint scratch of his stubble felt decadent, and I closed my eyes and allowed sensations to float over me.

His hands roved over my hips and waist, then dipped lower. It was only as one settled over my sex that I stiffened and my eyes flew open. He sensed my hesitance and stopped, his palm pressing lightly on my mound, my clit throbbing from the pressure. It was nice. Tempting. I arched, seeking more of the wonderful pressure, and his expression grew mischievous. He took his hand away, but just as I was about to complain, he touched two clever fingers to my softness and rubbed teasingly. I bit my lip and sought out more. I could feel my dampness soaking the fabric of the panties and would have been embarrassed if he hadn't groaned.

"You're really ready for it, aren't you?"

I nodded. "I told you."

"You did," he agreed. "But you were tense. Now you're not." His eyes shone nearly black in the flickering light. "You're going to feel so damn good. Can I strip you?"

"Yes."

He pulled off my panties, his expression warding off any fears about how I might measure up. He clearly liked what he saw. "I want to lick you until you scream my name."

"Please," I asked, widening my legs shamelessly. No one had ever done that before, but it sounded wonderful. "Oh!"

He licked a stripe with his hot tongue along my center, and my hips bucked of their own volition. My eyes squeezed shut as he set his mouth to me and made the kind of hungry sound I'd no doubt hear in my dreams for years to come.

"Oh, yes, yes, oh my God." I clutched his hair, unable to control the sounds spilling from me. "Please, I need you, ungh."

I shuddered, pressing closer, so near to the edge, but then an unfamiliar sensation brought me back to earth. It wasn't bad, as such, just different. An intrusion. I glanced down and saw that Liam had thrust a finger inside me. He was watching me carefully.

"Okay?"

"Um, yes." I didn't sound totally convincing, but when he crooked his finger and my internal muscles all pulsed and heated at once, I moaned. Okay, I definitely liked it.

He teased me back to the edge. Then, when I was teetering on the brink, he left for a few seconds, rifling through our packs for the condoms that we'd brought just in case. I think we both knew where tonight was leading.

There was a crackle of foil as he tore it open, and then he was straddling me, his cock hard and so much bigger than his finger.

"You want this?" he asked, giving me plenty of time to respond.

"Yes," I replied softly, safe in the knowledge that if I'd said no, he'd have backed off. That was all I needed to be sure he'd take care of me.

"Thank you for trusting me." His voice was thick with emotion, and he gave me a fierce look before positioning himself at my entrance and easing in. "Let me know if you need me to stop."

I focused on the strange sensation as he stretched and filled me. There was a dull burn as he slowly eased himself all the way inside.

"Hold still," I said. He stopped immediately, allowing me to adjust. I took a few slow, deep breaths, and the pain eased. I rocked my hips experimentally, and pleasure licked along my nerves. I did it again and smiled at the delicious sensations that rocketed through me. "Okay, you can move."

He found a slow rhythm, and we moved together languidly. There was no rush. None of the desperation of earlier. When my orgasm began to build, it was slow and deep. It felt strangely like our relationship: as if it was meant to last. I worked my hips, trembling as I crested, feeling like I'd been turned inside out in the best possible way. I clutched Liam's back and whispered his name. He groaned and jerked as he came. Before he collapsed on top of me, he met my eyes and pressed a tender kiss to my lips. My heart lurched.

I was officially crazy about Liam Braddock.

Chapter Eight

KENNEDY

The week after Liam and I first made love was like a dream. Whenever we're weren't working, we were together at my cottage, learning the different ways our bodies could enjoy each other. We were insatiable. Deepening our physical relationship seemed to have also deepened our emotional connection. When we were together, I was so attuned to him, and when we were apart, I'd sometimes think of him and smile, only to receive a text seconds later that he'd experienced the same thing. For the first time I could remember, I felt settled. Everything was as it was meant to be.

On Saturday evening, we were celebrating his father, Eugene's, fiftieth birthday at the local pub, Drunken Destiny, which Eugene and Heather, Liam's mother, owned. Eugene was officially off duty tonight, and the Braddock family had spent the afternoon readying the pub, which would be closed to the public—but from what I could tell, basically open to any local who might care to wander in and wish him a happy birthday. The bar staff were volunteering their time because they apparently liked their boss that much. Although to be fair, I could relate. I'd gotten really lucky in working for Tabitha. I'd finally summoned the courage to ask about the possibility of selling postcards from her shop, and she'd put in an order already. Now I just needed to get them printed and shipped to the resort.

I donned the dress I'd chosen for the night, a slinky black number with a scandalously low-cut back and a deceptively prim front. I'd never been one for flashing my body around, since I tended to be a little on the shy side and hadn't really gone through a rebellious phase—unless this counted—but it didn't worry me if people saw my back, and the dress was going to drive Liam out of his mind. Worth it. I'd already done my makeup, but I checked my reflection in the bedroom mirror just to make sure I hadn't smudged anything.

"Kennedy," Grace called from the other room. We'd planned to walk to the pub together. Fortunately, it wasn't far, so I'd chosen a pair of sexy black pumps to accompany the dress.

"In here," I called back. "You can come through."

A moment later, she appeared in the doorway. "You look beautiful."

"Thanks." I fastened a silver necklace around my throat and took a moment to look at her. "So do you."

At twenty-two, Grace felt more like a friend than my landlord. She was pretty in a quiet, refined fashion, with dark tresses that fell almost to her waist, a slender neck, and long legs that made her tall enough to rival most men for height. She had sharp cheekbones and an elegant way of carrying herself. She wouldn't have been out of place on the cover of *Vogue* or as a member of an aristocratic family. It was crazy to think she'd been raised by her quirky, palm-reading aunt.

Tonight, Grace was wearing a classy dress in a shade of

forest green that brought out the highlights in her hazel eyes. She didn't have a jacket on even though it was cool outside, but I'd learned that she didn't feel the cold much. I grabbed a pink jacket and pulled it on over my dress. I'd need it until we arrived at the pub. I stuffed my wallet into the jacket pocket and joined Grace.

We locked the cottage and wandered down the pavement together. Lights shone from the vintage lamp posts that lined Centennial Street as we made our way past shops that had already closed for the weekend. Drunken Destiny was at the end of the block. A warm glow emanated from it, and I could hear voices as we approached. Grace and I had been there a couple of hours ago, helping prepare, but while the Braddock siblings had stayed to add the finishing touches, we'd slipped away to have a quick dinner, wash up, and make ourselves presentable.

As we entered, a few people glanced up and greeted us. Grace gave me a smile and headed over to join Nate and a couple of their other friends. I found Eugene up front, talking to the bartender. He was handsome for an older guy, with salt-and-pepper hair, a creased face, and twinkling blue eyes. I imagined Liam would look similar when he was that age.

"Happy birthday, Eugene." I wrung my hands awkwardly. He'd insisted on not getting any gifts, but it felt wrong to show up empty-handed.

"Thanks, Kennedy." He clapped my shoulder and smiled. "In my mind, I'm not a day over thirty, but then I look in the mirror and see my dad looking back at me."

"Your dad is looking good," Heather said, appearing behind him and pinching his bum.

I stifled a giggle. I loved the way Eugene and Heather acted around each other. Playful and loving, even after more than twenty-five years and six children together.

"Shush, woman." He silenced her with a kiss. Someone whistled. They separated, and Eugene kissed the tip of her nose, then gestured toward one of the tables that fronted onto what was now a dance floor. We'd cleared out the pool tables earlier, and someone had strung lights up while I'd been gone. "Liam is over there."

"Thanks." I headed over, finding him beside his best friend, Asher, the paramedic who'd treated me the day Liam and I had met. I'd discovered he and Liam were almost inseparable. Asher was cockier and more outgoing than Liam, but he and I still got along well. To be honest, he was probably the sort of person who got on with everyone.

"Kenz!"

I spotted Liam's younger sister, Summer, on the opposite side of the table. She was a precocious fourteen-year-old, and she seemed to have gone all-out in a dress I was surprised her brothers had let her leave the house in. Although, knowing her, she'd have sneaked it over here earlier and changed at the last minute so no one had a chance to suggest she wear something else. She'd done her makeup too, and based on the way she'd angled herself toward Asher, I wondered if it was supposed to be for his benefit. I winced at the thought. I couldn't blame Summer if she had a crush on her brother's hot best friend, but she had to know nothing was ever going to happen there. Asher treated her like a baby sister.

"Hey, Summer," I said, greeting Liam with a kiss and then sinking onto the chair beside his sister. Music was playing, but there weren't many people on the dance floor. "Nice dress."

She beamed. "I borrowed it from Bailey. You look good too."

"You really do," Liam rumbled, running his eyes over me appreciatively.

"Ew," Summer said, pulling a face. "Young ears are listening."

He smirked. "I don't see any young ears around here. Surely nobody young would be wearing a dress like that. The sort of mature lady who'd wear that dress would be used to hearing their very handsome brother woo his girlfriend."

Summer huffed. Their interplay made me smile. I loved the way they teased each other, and they seemed to have incorporated me into their ranks. I felt like part of the family. I'd been thinking more about the possibility of staying in Destiny Falls, and while I knew I'd miss my own family like crazy, it might be worth the sacrifice if it meant I got to keep Liam and become part of the Braddock inner circle.

"Want to dance?" Liam asked as the song changed to something slow, turning away from his sister.

"I'd like that." I stood, remembering my high heels at the last moment, but surely I'd be able to manage dancing in them with such a slow beat, and if I had to take them off, I don't think anyone would bat an eyelid. They were a casual crowd.

I shucked my jacket and draped it over the chair, then let Liam lead me onto the dance floor. He encircled me with his arms, his eyes flaring as he felt my bare skin. His palm traced up and down my back, measuring how much was exposed.

"Sexy," he murmured.

I just smiled and rested my cheek on his chest as he drew me closer. We swayed, moving in a small circle, our steps in perfect union. He made a contented sound deep in his chest, and it vibrated against my cheek. I could hear his heartbeat, slow and steady. My stomach twisted at the thought of how much capacity for love that big heart of his had. I'd never met anyone like him. He cared deeply, and he wasn't afraid to show it.

Time for me to be fearless too.

I tipped my head back and met his gaze. "I love you."

The emotion that passed over his face made my bravery feel worth it, ten times over.

"You're incredible," he said, soft enough that the words didn't venture beyond the bubble that seemed to surround us. "I didn't think I'd be able to open my heart again so easily, but then you came along, and it's like we just fit together. I love you too."

December

Chapter Nine

LIAM

"Are we nearly there?" Kennedy puffed as we traipsed up rough dirt stairs cut into a path through the thinning forest.

"Just a little further," I told her. We were somewhere up the side of Destiny Peak. I'd been wanting to bring her to this spot for a while, but I'd been waiting for ideal weather so she'd get the best first impression of it.

The summer air was warm, and cicadas chirped as the last of the forest cleared, and we entered a sunny plateau with golden tussock rippling in the breeze. I marched to the edge where a rock formed a clifftop that overlooked the entire township of Destiny Falls and much of the surrounding areas. Thanks to the perfectly cloudless sky, we could see for miles.

"Oh, wow." Kennedy drew up beside me, still breathing heavily. Awe filled her voice. "That's stunning."

I smiled. "It's one of my favorite places to come and think. Or just enjoy being alive."

I sat on a rock positioned several yards back from the

edge and patted the neighboring one, indicating for her to join me. She lowered herself onto it, wincing, presumably as her sore muscles twinged. She slid the day pack off her shoulders and dug around for a banana, then passed me a protein bar. I sipped from my water bottle before taking a bite, and we stayed silent while we caught our breath. It had been quite a hike up to the lookout.

"I can see why you were so concerned with making sure the sky was clear when we came here," she said, shielding her eyes with her hand as she looked out. "It's amazing."

Happiness fizzed in my gut and went to my head, making me feel light as air. "I'm happy you like it. My favorite thing about being here is that I can look out over pretty much everything and everyone I care about." Below, in the distance, the streets of Destiny Falls township formed thin ribbons, and I imagined my parents walking along Centennial Street, hand in hand, or Asher playing cards with Igor and Zone in the fire station. The pub. The school. The home where I'd learned to walk, ride a bike, and tie my shoes. "This view reminds me of why I love Destiny Falls so much. I could never be happy anywhere else."

I glanced over at Kennedy and saw emotion sparkling in her vibrant eyes.

"Destiny Falls is kinda great." Her voice shook a little. "I've been thinking more about moving here after my one-year contract with the resort is done." She caught her lower lip between her teeth. "But I don't want to put any pressure on you or our relationship. I haven't made a final decision yet. I just want you to know I'm seriously considering it."

I wanted so badly to tell her I hoped she would move here that I practically vibrated out of my skin, but I managed to keep my mouth shut. She needed to make the decision herself, and she needed all the facts. I wouldn't be able to stand it if she moved here and then left again a few months later. She'd still only been in town for six months. She might have a rosy view of the limitations of living in a small mountain community.

"Just remember that we're isolated out here," I said. "There are no clubs, not many shops, and only a couple of places you can buy food." All things Zoe had complained about. "There's no hospital and not a lot of people our own age. Not to mention there aren't a heap of things to do."

Kennedy's expression wavered. "If you don't want me to move here, just say it."

"No," I exclaimed, horrified she could think that. "That's not it at all. I just want you to know what you'll be missing out on."

"Liam." She gave me a meaningful look. "I come from L.A. Even the biggest city in New Zealand is smaller than my hometown. I know exactly what the differences are between here and somewhere urban. Trust me."

"Okay, when you put it like that, I feel like an idiot. I'm sorry."

"It's all right." She leaned over to kiss me. "My fully informed opinion so far is that the benefits of Destiny Falls more than make up for its shortcomings."

Joy sang in my veins as I finally allowed myself to believe her.

Kennedy loved me, and she loved my home. Everything was shaping up exactly how I wanted it to. My mouth stretched so wide my jaw ached, but I couldn't stop smiling.

Kennedy pulled out her camera and snapped a photo of me. She wandered to the edge of the cliff and took several pictures of the view. Then she perched on the rock beside me again and shifted as close as possible, fitting us both into the camera frame. At the last moment, before the flash went off, she turned and brushed her lips against my cheek.

I couldn't imagine a more perfect moment.

51

April

Chapter Ten

LIAM

"I can't believe you've been in Destiny Falls for nearly a year and haven't actually visited the waterfall," I said to Kennedy as we paced the well-worn track that started at an unpaved parking area behind Destiny Fibers, the shop Grace's aunt Desdemona owned. Further up, the trail would branch out, with the falls in one direction and the tarn further along.

Kennedy shrugged. "I've heard the mythology of the falls. It seemed wrong to go alone."

I was silently pleased because that would make it more special for us to go together. "Tell me what you've heard about the background story."

I watched her ass as we walked, trying to distract myself from what was to come. My heart had been racing all day, and now that we were less than half an hour from the big moment, my palms were sweating, and I could hardly catch my breath. Fortunately, if Kennedy asked, I could blame it on the invigorating hike.

She glanced over her shoulder. "Just that a pair of star-crossed lovers secretly got married there, having eloped.

Supposedly she was engaged to marry someone else because her parents didn't approve of her beau?"

I nodded. "Rumor has it, they lived a long and happy life somewhere far away from here. But their epic love story started with the illicit wedding at the falls. The minister who performed the ceremony was later shunned by local society."

"Wow."

"Right?" I wasn't sure if the story was historically accurate. It had probably been embellished with each retelling, but Destiny Falls was the place everybody wanted to come to pledge their love, so it hadn't done the township any harm. Truth be told, I kind of liked it. I was a romantic at heart. "Shh. Listen." We were close enough to the falls to hear the rush of water. "We're nearly there."

Kennedy unfastened her camera from a sling around her neck and held it as we came around a bend in the path. My breath hitched. No matter how many times I saw it, the view never got old. A pool of blue-tinged water surrounded the base of the waterfall. In summer, many people swam here, but it was too cold for that now. At the end of the pool, water cascaded down a moss-covered rockface. The waterfall was like something from an Irish faerie glen. It had a dreamlike quality. Lush and ethereal at the same time. Above the rockface, the fall was tiered, with three small steps carved by nature.

"Oh my God."

I wrapped my arms around her from behind. "Beautiful, isn't it?"

"Amazing." Her eyes were wide. "I can't believe you didn't insist I come here sooner."

I laughed. "I had to get the timing right."

"For what?" She turned in my arms.

"This." With shaking hands, I withdrew a small box from my pocket and offered it to her. She tucked her camera away and took it. "Maybe it's a bit cliche, but I wanted to bring you here to ask you an important question. Don't worry, it's not a ring." We'd already discussed the fact that neither of us wanted to marry until we were older.

I rubbed my lips together, my heart in my throat. Kennedy was returning to L.A. soon. Not for good. She planned to come back to Destiny Falls once she had everything in order, but I was terrified she'd leave and that would be the end of it. After Zoe, I was gun-shy. I might love Destiny Falls with every fiber of my being, but not everyone felt the same.

"Open it."

She did, her fingers clumsy as they fumbled with the lid. Inside, nestled on a bed of velvet, was a key.

She raised her eyes. "What's this?"

"Kennedy, I love you." I heard the quaver in my voice and hoped she didn't notice it. "I'd like you to move in with me when you come back. This is a key to my place."

Her lips parted and a breath gusted from between them. "Really?"

There was a hint of something in her tone. Hope? Excitement?

"Yes. I want the key to be a reminder of everything that's waiting for you while you're gone. What do you say?"

She threw her arms around my neck and hugged me tight. "A million times, yes!"

Thank God.

I drew her in for a kiss. "We've pledged it in front of the falls. No takesies backsies."

She smiled indulgently. "There isn't a universe in which I could ever want to be apart from you. Mythical pledge or not, that doesn't change. I love you."

Chapter Eleven

KENNEDY

As I navigated the streets of L.A. two weeks later, I was recalling the way Liam had smiled and kissed me at the waterfall. My chest ached from missing him, but I knew that within another couple of weeks, I'd be back in his arms. The separation had only served to make me more certain of where I belonged. Unfortunately, it took a bit of organizing to permanently uproot my life and move it several thousand miles across the ocean. Explaining my decision to Mom and Malcolm hadn't been easy. I knew they'd hoped they'd have me back but they'd accepted my choice and said they wanted me to be happy. Since then, I'd been getting my paperwork in order, and I had offloaded almost all of the possessions I no longer needed or wanted.

A Lorde song came onto the radio and I sang along, heading for my family's home in Bel Air. Hearing the singer reminded me of Liam. Nearly everything reminded me of Liam lately. A smile crept over my face. He was going to be so pleased when my flight finally landed. I knew he trusted me, but it was difficult for him to let go of that last remnant of concern that I might abandon him. I couldn't wait to see his expression when he realized for certain that our future together was happening.

I turned a corner and slowed, frowning at the flashing lights up ahead. A police car sat outside our gates, a pair of officers waiting to be let in. I pulled up behind them and pushed the remote control to open the gate. Malcolm had had it installed, along with a high surrounding fence and a state of the art security system, because he was an agent to the rich and famous.

The police car circled the small garden and parked near the entrance to the house. I wondered idly what they thought of it, and whether they'd treat us in a certain way because of where we lived. When I'd first moved here with Blair and Mom a little over ten years ago, I'd been intimidated. The place was practically a mansion. But after being here so long, it had stopped being scary. Instead, I'd filled it with memories of playing with my siblings, helping them with their homework, and sharing meals. Now, it was just home.

But why were the police here?

Had there been a break-in? It seemed unlikely.

Perhaps Blair had gotten into trouble. He was going through a rebellious stage. The other kids were too young to have done anything to warrant police intervention. Unless, of course, one of them had been abducted.

My heart clattered against my ribcage as I parked behind them and got out of the car on shaky legs. All it took was one look at the lead officer's face to know they'd come with bad news.

"What is it?" I asked, my pulse thundering in my ears. "What's going on?"

"Miss Kennedy Carter?" the female officer asked, her expression full of sympathy.

"Yes, that's me." My voice was growing shrill. "Is someone hurt? One of the kids?"

The other officer gestured toward the house. "Why don't we go inside?"

"No." My legs refused to cooperate. "I need to know."

The female officer touched my shoulder. I flinched back. "Kennedy, you should make yourself comfortable. Are your siblings home?"

"I think so, but I'll need to check."

"Okay." She nodded. "Let's go in and you can gather the others."

I didn't want to. I wanted to kick the police off the property so I didn't have to hear what they had to say. But clapping my hands over my ears wouldn't make whatever news they planned to share go away. It would only buy me a little time to be in denial.

"After you." She indicated for me to lead the way.

My legs barely functioned correctly as I walked across the parking area, up the stairs, and then tested the handle. The door was locked, which must mean Mom and Malcolm were still out. They'd left me in charge, and I'd delegated to Blair when I had to run an errand. Blair might have an attitude problem, but he was careful about keeping our younger siblings safe.

I slotted my key into the lock and entered, automatically removing my shoes and lining them up beside the others. To my surprise, both officers did the same. I gestured through a door to the left.

"That's the living room. I'll get the others and be with you soon. Can I bring you a cup of coffee?" Anything to delay the inevitable.

"No, thank you," the male officer said.

I jogged up the stairs to the first floor where the bedrooms were and knocked on each door. "Come on, kids. We've got guests."

Blair emerged first, his guitar tucked under his arm. "Everything's fine," he said a little sullenly. "I've been checking up on them."

Mina's head popped through another doorway. "Do I have to come?" she whined. "My book is in a really good spot."

"The police are downstairs," I told her, watching her eyes light with interest. My half sister was obsessed with the criminal justice system. She was always reading mystery books meant for older kids.

"The police?" Jamie and Joel chorused in tandem, bouncing out from the den, both wearing pajamas even though it was midday. "Are they here to arrest someone?"

God, I hoped not.

"I don't know, Jamie. Why don't we go down and ask them?"

"Okay!" He raced down the stairs with Joel at his heels.

"Careful, boys," I called. One of these days, they were going to trip and injure themselves.

Mina stepped out of her room and followed them at a more measured pace.

"You sure you have no idea what this is about?" I asked Blair quietly.

"What? You think I've been breaking the law?" He sounded offended. "I'm a misunderstood musician, not a thug."

I held my hands up in a gesture of peace, but I couldn't help wondering... if it wasn't that, and nothing had happened to the kids, then what had brought them here? An icy shiver ran down my spine. I didn't think I wanted to know the answer.

I dropped by the kitchen to collect Ingrid, who kept the house tidy and the children fed when Mom wasn't here. We gathered in the living room.

"Please, sit," the female officer said.

I sank onto the edge of the sofa, wishing the boys were still young enough that they'd climb onto my knee for cuddles. I could use the physical comfort. Unfortunately, they'd decided that eight was too old for snuggles.

"I'm Officer Rush, and this is Officer Needham." The woman took a deep breath, and I dug my fingertips into my palms, using the tiny pricks of pain to ground myself. "I'm very sorry to have to tell you this, but a little over an hour ago, your parents were involved in an accident. They passed away before they could be taken to hospital."

"No," I gasped. It wasn't possible. I'd seen Mom and Malcolm only this morning, and they'd been in perfect health, laughing and joking as they prepared for the day.

"You're lying," Blair spat, lunging to his feet.

"I'm afraid not." Officer Needham stepped forward to stand beside his partner. "We were at the scene of the accident before coming here."

"They… gone?" My brain couldn't make sense of that. "You must have made a mistake."

"I'm sorry, Miss Carter, but there's no mistake."

Beside me, Mina started to cry softly. Ingrid embraced her. The younger boys didn't seem to fully understand what was going on. They stared at each other, upset but confused, not able to comprehend that their parents might simply be dead.

Just like that. With no warning.

I was more than ten years older, and I wasn't even sure I understood it myself.

"You're absolutely certain?" Ingrid asked, stroking Mina's hair.

"Yes, Ma'am."

The bottom fell out of my world.

I could hear voices, but my brain wouldn't process them. Movement around me seemed jerky and disjointed. When I tried to focus on Blair, I felt dizzy. My head spun.

Somehow, I found myself across the room, in front of the police officers, with Rush's hand on my shoulder. Her lips were moving, but the words made no sense. I heard something about support. Custody arrangements. Was there anyone they could call?

No. There's no one.

We had no extended family that I was aware of. It was just us, alone in the world.

My vision seemed to warp, everything moving painfully slowly, and then all at once.

We're alone.

Suddenly, I wasn't a girl about to move thousands of miles for love. I'd been plunged into a nightmare reality where my parents, who I'd loved with my whole heart, were dead and I wasn't just babysitting the kids while they were out for the day.

I was responsible for these children. Solely responsible. Unless Mom and Malcolm had named another guardian in a will. Did they even have a will? I'd never asked. I hadn't wanted to know, and I'd thought there were plenty of years before they'd need to worry about something like that.

Officer Rush's face was right in front of me. She seemed to be saying something, but I couldn't hear past the pressure building in my ears.

Breathe, Kennedy.

Something about a lawyer. A funeral. They were so sorry for our loss.

I watched my world fall down around me, knowing there was nothing I could do to stop it.

Chapter Twelve

LIAM

The phone rang and rang, but Kennedy didn't pick up.

"Answer, damn it," I growled.

I was going out of my mind with worry. She was supposed to be coming back to New Zealand soon, but her messages over the past two weeks had been infrequent and impersonal, and she hadn't answered a single one of my calls. Subconsciously, I was afraid my worst fears were coming true, but Kennedy wouldn't do that to me, would she? She loved me, and before now, she hadn't given me any reason to doubt her.

I dialed again and listened to the ring tone.

"Pick up, Kenz. Please pick up."

I raked my hand through my hair in frustration. Fuck, I was going to go bald if I didn't get to talk to her sooner or later. Pacing across my living room, I stared at the window into the front yard I'd hoped to share with the woman who was currently ignoring me. I'd imagined little boys and girls playing on that lawn while Kennedy sat nearby, her camera on her knee as she watched them. Desperation squeezed my chest so tight it hurt.

"Hello."

I nearly dropped the phone. She'd answered.

"Kennedy. I'm so happy to hear you." The pressure on my chest eased, and I felt like I could breathe again. "I've been so worried. Is everything all right?"

"No, it's not." Her voice cracked on the last word. She sounded as though she'd been crying. "Everything is wrong."

I felt a twinge in my heart. I hated the despair and defeat lacing her tone. "What's going on, baby? Tell me."

She sniffled, and released a hiccupping sob. "You're going to hate me."

"Never," I vowed, even as my stomach churned with fear. "It's not possible. Please tell me what's happened."

She took a shuddering breath. "Things have changed. I've decided to stay in L.A."

My mouth slackened, and my free hand fell to my side. "What? No. Why? Is it your parents? Did they put you up to this? Talk to me, Kenz."

For a long moment, she didn't speak, and then I realized she was silently crying.

"If someone tried to push you into staying, don't let them," I insisted. "Remember how happy you were here."

There was another wet sniff, and then she came through loud and clear. "It's not my parents. This is all coming from me. I can't move away from my family. They need me."

"But I need you too," I said in disbelief. "You love it here. You love me. I know you do."

"I'm really sorry to hurt you." Her voice was tight and watery. "I wish it didn't have to happen this way."

"It doesn't." My mind raced as I thought through the options. I didn't understand what was going on. Sure, I'd been worried about her silence, but I hadn't seen this coming. Despite the niggles of fear, deep down I'd trusted her. "Are you breaking up with me?"

"Yes," she whispered. "I can't do this anymore. I'm sorry, but you and Destiny Falls just aren't in my future."

My mouth clapped shut.

Oh no, not again.

I finally got it. I was being dumped by a city girl who'd decided that a country boy and his quiet hometown weren't good enough for her. It was Zoe all over again.

At least Kennedy had the guts to say it to my face.

But I wasn't going to give up easily. We had something special.

"I'll fly over there," I said. "I'll book a flight right now, and when I get to L.A., we can talk about it. If you really hate the idea of coming back here, maybe I can move there. At least give me the chance to think about it." I couldn't stomach the thought of leaving the place that was so much a part of me, and for anyone else, I wouldn't even make the offer, but Kennedy might be worth the sacrifice.

She laughed bitterly. "You'd hate L.A. You've said a thousand times how much you loathe the city, and that Destiny Falls is the only place you could be happy."

"Yeah, but that was when I thought I could have you *and* be in Destiny Falls. Now you're telling me I have to choose. Let me decide for myself which choice I want to make."

"I'm not asking you to choose." Her tone was heavy, but firm. "We're over. I know that's not what you wanted. It's not what I wanted either. But it is what it is." I opened my mouth to argue, but she continued, "The life you're offering can't make me happy, and the one I'm offering would make you miserable. There's no point dragging it out. Let's cut our losses."

The life you're offering can't make me happy.

Whoever wrote that rhyme about "sticks and stones

can break my bones but words can never hurt me" clearly never had their heart torn apart by a woman, because this hurt like hell.

"Is that really what you want?" I asked.

"It is."

The fact I didn't hear any doubt in her voice flayed me.

"Okay, then. Guess it's over."

I hung up and stared blindly at the phone. At her name on the screen.

I rubbed my chest, but couldn't dull the pain. If she'd hit me with a truck, she couldn't have hurt me more.

Everything had been perfect. I'd finally allowed myself to believe in our happily ever after, only to have the rug pulled out from under me.

I threw my phone across the room. It hit the wall and shattered,

I tossed my head back and shouted every curse word in my vocabulary.

I felt hollow inside. Empty and used up.

Kennedy wasn't coming back. She didn't want me enough to leave her home and move halfway around the world to the middle of nowhere. I'd been a fool to ever have believed she could.

Now I was a heartbroken fool.

Chapter Thirteen

KENNEDY

My lower lip wobbled and another round of tears crashed over me. Self-loathing and self-pity twisted unpleasantly through my veins. I'd just ended things with the love of my life, and now his last memory of me would be this awful conversation in which I'd probably made him think he wasn't worth the discomfort of permanently leaving my home. That couldn't be further from the truth. He was worth so much more, and right now, cold and alone in the bedroom of a house I apparently owned, I wanted more than anything to bury my face in his strong chest and have him hold me. I wanted him to murmur soft nothings in my ear, but I didn't deserve that.

I'd hurt him.

I'd never wanted to cause him pain. After everything we'd been through, all the promises we'd made, I'd broken him. And now, I was the one breaking.

It wasn't as though I'd had any choice though. My siblings needed me more than he did. I had to step up without any fuss, for their sake. I was the only guardian they had left.

I hadn't wanted to break up with Liam, but doing so was the best thing for him when I knew how much Destiny Falls meant to him, and how much he'd struggle if he came to L.A.

If I'd told him everything and asked him to move, he'd either have ended our relationship anyway—which would have devastated me when I was already feeling low—or, more likely, he'd have felt obligated to uproot everything and make himself miserable by joining me. At least this way, he could eventually be happy again. Meanwhile, I'd deal with the fallout of my parents' deaths without burdening him. I'd always managed to shoulder responsibility before, and there was no reason why this should be different.

"Kennedy!" one of the twins called from the hall outside my room. "Mina is crying again."

I buried my face in my palms at the reminder of how out of my depth I really was. I didn't know how to stop Mina crying. I didn't know how to fix things for any of them. Blair had been walking around like a zombie, hardly eating, then sitting up all night on his guitar. Mina cried and cried, her eyes constantly red and swollen. The boys were fighting more than they used to, and it seemed like the tiniest thing would set them off.

Somehow, I had to get them through their grief. I could do it. I knew I could. I just wasn't sure how yet. But I *would*.

A nonverbal teenager, a devastated preteen, and a pair of angry and confused little boys were depending on me.

We had no other family. No loving aunt or uncle to take us in. It was down to me to raise these kids and protect them from either being thrown into the foster system or palmed off on some distant relative none of them had ever met. Yes, we were wealthy, thanks to an inheritance from Malcolm, but we were also alone.

So very alone.

The call came again. "Kennedy!"

"I'll be there in a minute." My voice was raw.

I went to the bed and carefully wrapped the scrapbook I'd created, that chronicled my relationship with Liam, in cloth, then carried it to the closet and placed it on a shelf at the top, just out of sight. I'd made it as a surprise for him, but now he'd never see it. Never know how much I loved him.

I swallowed another sob and positioned the box containing his key beside the scrapbook. I couldn't bring myself to get rid of it because that would mean throwing out everything it symbolized.

Hope. Love. A future with him.

It has to be this way, I reminded myself. *It's best for every-one... other than me.*

I couldn't uproot my family after such a massive loss and move them all the way across the world, away from the only home they'd ever known. Just like I couldn't leave them to the whims of some distant relative or the foster system, or drag Liam away from the home he loved and thrust him into a world of chaos and grief.

I shut the closet door and turned away from my memories. Straightening my shoulders, I walked out into the hall to deal with the mess my family had become, leaving my future with Liam Braddock behind.

11 Years Later

Epilogue (Present)

KENNEDY

I'd just finished herding Jamie, Joel, and their college hockey teammates into the living room so Ingrid could clean up after lunch when my phone rang. I glanced down and realized I'd already missed one call from my former costar and now best friend, Gray, whom I'd acted in several movies with. I closed the door behind me, muting the noise coming from over a dozen jocks, and accepted the call with video.

"Hi, sorry about that," I said "I had to get to another room. The twins are here with some of their friends, and it's madness."

Gray smiled. He was a handsome guy, nearly ten years older than me, with golden brown eyes and a few gray flecks in his dark hair. "That's fine," he said. "I was just calling to check in and see how things are going with the security, and with you in general."

My lips twisted. I'd confessed some concerns to him a while ago about a potential stalker situation. I was yet to have any hard proof, but my gut told me the threat was real and that I wasn't just dealing with some overenthusi-astic fan of my acting career.

"Are you worried about me, Gray?" I asked

He held up his thumb and forefinger an inch apart. "A little."

"Thanks for calling." I couldn't seem to summon a smile or any words to put his mind at ease. Gray had once been the victim of a stalker himself. The stalker had burned his house down, and his housekeeper had died in the blaze.

I pursed my lips. Perhaps I should have kept my concerns to myself. I should have known that sharing would only worry him, and he had enough on his mind without me adding to it. "Like I told you, the security system is set up. They added measures around the perimeter of the property as well as for the house itself. I've taken a bodyguard on a couple of outings, but honestly, it's easier to just not go anywhere."

Gray nodded. "Don't let them rule your life though, Kenz."

I glanced away, checking to make sure none of the men in the other room would be able to hear. "Why not?" I asked quietly. "It's not as if I'm calling most of the shots anyway."

It was a fact of life that actresses mostly went where and when they were told by directors, agents, managers, or whoever else was in charge that day. It was rare for me to have an entire twenty-four hours under my own control.

"Let's not talk about me anymore," I suggested, feeling bad for bringing his mood down. "I want to hear all about how things are going with you and Mikayla."

Mikayla was new his love interest. I wasn't sure if she'd reached girlfriend status yet or not.

"Better than I ever could have imagined. But don't change the subject." He studied me, looking so deep, I felt like he was peeling back layers I hadn't exposed for years. I wasn't sure what he could see there. I intentionally kept that shit under lock and key.

He sighed, hesitated, then asked, "When was the last time you were truly happy?"

The question hit me like a punch in the solar plexus, driving the air from me. God, who asked something like that?

My lower lip quivered.

Pull yourself together, I mentally ordered, but it didn't do any good. I sniffled, and a tear leaked out of one eye and trailed down my cheek.

"Oh, Kenz, I'm sorry," he said. "God, I wish I was there to give you a hug. I love you, and you don't need to answer that question. I had no right to ask it."

My lips parted, and I tried to think of what to say, but my mind was blank. When *was* the last time I'd been happy? I couldn't even remember.

Sure, I'd been satisfied with a job well done. Pleased when one of my siblings succeeded. But when was the last time I'd experienced that bone-deep sense of contentment that told a person all was right with their world? Had I ever felt it at all?

"Oh, wow," I choked out eventually. "I-I wasn't expecting that."

"I'm sorry," he repeated. "Ignore me."

"No." I swiped at the tears that were flowing freely down my face with the back of my hand. "I'm glad you asked."

Even if I didn't necessarily have an answer. But then a memory struck me. Liam Braddock and me, standing at a lookout on the side of Destiny Peak. Then another of Liam and me at Destiny Falls as he haltingly asked me to move in with him and offered me a key. I'd been happy then. Really, honestly happy.

"You are?" Gray looked uncertain.

"Yeah. I think…." I pondered those memories. Considered what they meant. "I've had plenty of happy times over the past decade or so, but I think the last time I was truly happy and free to be myself was when I was in New Zealand, living in Destiny Falls and dating Liam." My voice broke as I said my ex-boyfriend's name. A sob burst from me as reality hit with all the subtlety of a bomb. "That was eleven years ago, Gray. Have I really been unhappy for eleven years?"

"Not always," he said. "You've had good times, remember? Just like you mentioned before."

I put a hand to my mouth and hauled in a deep breath, then another. I nodded. "Yes, you're right." I gave a watery laugh. "God, I'm a mess today. Sorry for falling apart on you."

It was all this stress from always being on alert and wondering if someone was watching.

"Hey," he said sharply. "Never be sorry for that. I'm always here for you." He paused, then added, "Keep it in mind that your siblings are grown now. Jamie and Joel are living in a frat house for most of the year, right? And Mina is renting an apartment with some friends?"

"Yes." I frowned, not sure where he was going with this. "So?"

"Well…." He drew the word out. "If you need to leave L.A. for a while, you can. There's nothing tying you there now. Your siblings are adults, and while I don't know your full financial situation, I'm sure you have enough money to survive without working. Am I right?"

"You are." My tears dried up as I considered the implication. Could I actually do that? Pack up the life I'd built here and move on? Realistically, there was no reason I couldn't. "I guess I've been stuck here for so long that it didn't occur to me I was free again." I smiled tremulously. "Thanks for the reminder."

"No problem. If you ever need to fly to the bottom of the world to escape, my door is open."

He was sweet.

"I'm not sure Mikayla would appreciate that," I quipped, trying to lighten the moment.

At this, he grinned. "Mikayla would probably be more excited to see you than I would. Did you know that when we met, she had no idea who I was but fell all over herself when I told her we're friends?"

Despite the crazy thoughts whirling through my mind, I laughed. "I bet that was hard for your ego."

"Eh, could have been worse. In fact, it was kind of nice to have a clean slate with her."

"I bet." If I gave up the acting career I'd never really wanted and moved elsewhere, I could have a clean slate too. But nowhere else would be Destiny Falls. And nowhere else would have Liam. Perhaps what I needed wasn't a clean slate. It was the chance to make amends and reclaim the life I'd once wanted more than nearly anything.

There was a crash in the background, and I looked over my shoulder, cringing. Whenever the boys were home, something inevitably got damaged. They didn't seem to know their own size and strength. Especially Joel.

"Thanks for calling, but I'd better go. It sounds like Joel managed to break something again."

"See you," he said. "Good luck with damage control."

I hung up and hustled off to play the part of responsible older sister slash mom figure. I'd been doing it for so long, it had become second nature.

But now, Gray had challenged my usual cycle of thoughts. He was right. My siblings were adults. Young adults, sure, but fully able to care for themselves. I didn't love my job, and there was every possibility someone dangerous was following me around. Watching me.

Things didn't have to be this way. If I was brave enough, I might be able to have everything I'd once yearned for—even if it was over a decade later than planned. Could I do it? Could I give up everything I had and take a leap of blind faith?

Yes. I smiled. I rather thought I could.

THE END

Come Back to You Excerpt

KENNEDY

Hi Liam,

Yet another email I'll never send you.

I was offered an acting job yesterday by one of Malcolm's old clients. It's just a minor part. A fill-in, really, but it pays well. We're not hurting for money, but only a year after Malcolm and Mom died, I've already gone through a scary amount of what should be saved for the kids' college funds. Maybe I should start working to make sure I don't inadvertently limit their options. But then, is it better for them to have that money in the future, or for them to have me around 24/7 now?

I've got no idea. You'd know better than I would. Your family has always been so strong. I feel like I screw up every day, and I worry I won't give them what they need. I wish I could talk to you about it.

I miss you.

Love,

K xx

.   .   .

I drove into Destiny Falls as dusk was settling over the township. The last rays of sunlight gilded the colonial style shopfronts of Centennial Street in gold. To the right, an older lady wrapped in a fluffy purple jersey and a matching knit hat brought in the Open sign outside Destiny Fibers. I smiled. Desdemona Smith. It was nice to know some things hadn't changed.

The street was mostly empty of people, with a few gathered outside Drunken Destiny, which looked to have been repainted during the eleven years I'd been gone, and several others clustered around a cafe a couple of buildings down from Desdemona's shop. That was new. I glanced at signwriting on the window. Taste of Destiny. My lips curved into a smile. I'd always loved the way the locals played up to the town's name.

For a brief moment, I considered pulling over for a coffee. I'd flown from Los Angeles to New Zealand the day before yesterday, and then I'd been driving all day yesterday as well as today. Prior to leaving, I'd been rushing through a tourist Visa application. Now, I was exhausted and not in the mood to deal with the possibility of tourists at the cafe recognizing me. Being a successful actress had its perks—I never needed to worry about money again— but it had downsides too.

A shiver ran through me. *Serious* downsides.

Like the stalker who'd been hassling me with anonymous social media messages, disturbing videos, and had escalated to infiltrating my house. I still didn't know who the person was, but that shouldn't matter, since they'd surely never follow me halfway around the world— assuming they'd be able to locate me in the first place.

Not that the stalker was the reason I'd decided to return to Destiny Falls. They—and my friend, Gray—had just prompted me to look at my life, and I hadn't liked what I'd seen. Beneath the glitz and glam, I wasn't happy. Hadn't been in a long time. Blair, Mina, Joel, and Jamie had all moved out, so for once, I'd been able to put myself first and come back to the place my heart had yearned for since the accident that changed everything.

Back to the *man* I'd never stopped loving.

I didn't know anything about Liam's life now. He could be married with kids. He might have moved away, although I highly doubted it. He'd always been so determined to stay in Destiny Falls. Even if he was single and still in town, he probably wouldn't want anything to do with me. But I was no stranger to adversity. I'd raised my half-siblings when I wasn't much more than a child myself. I wasn't afraid of working hard for forgiveness and a second chance.

I pulled onto a side road and followed it for a couple of blocks until I arrived at the cottage I used to rent from Grace Smith, a woman a couple of years older than me. I scanned the outside. The weathered boards were the same shade of white they used to be, with no sign of wear and tear. Perhaps they'd been repainted over the years, or maybe Grace had simply maintained them in pristine condition. The door was a muted green with a metal flap for letters to be pushed through and an old-fashioned brass ringer. The tiled roof had the same cozy appeal that had once drawn me to it. In short, it looked like I'd never left.

Pocketing the keys, I got out of the car and headed for the main house. As far as I could tell, Grace still ran the operation here. I'd made my booking through an automated online system under a different name—partly because I was worried she'd cancel it if she knew who I really was and partly because it was just good sense to do that as a celebrity. Hopefully Grace wouldn't be too angry about the deception. I paused for a moment to gather my courage, then pressed the doorbell. I could hear it ring through the house, and I gnawed on my lower lip, preparing for a hostile welcome.

The door swung inward, and there she was, as beautiful as I remembered. Her face had more maturity, but nothing else seemed to have changed. I fought the urge to hug her, knowing she probably wouldn't return the affection.

Her smile faltered, and she stopped abruptly, crossing her arms over her chest. "Let me guess. Katy?"

I winced. "I'm sorry."

She shook her head. "I never thought I'd see you again. Not after all this time."

I shifted from one foot to the other, unable to read her. She clearly wasn't pleased, but she didn't seem furious either. More… cautious.

"Things changed," I said, knowing the weak excuse couldn't possibly sum up the many ways in which my life had been tipped upside down over the past decade. I'd need hours to explain the whole painful story. "I can leave if you don't want me here."

Grace pursed her lips and was quiet for a long moment with her hand on the door, effectively barring me from entering the house. She searched my eyes. I didn't know what she hoped to find, but I held her gaze.

Eventually, she spoke. "If you're expecting to be welcomed back with open arms, you're going to be disappointed."

I released a bitter laugh. "I know. Believe me."

"People are going to be upset," she continued, her tone level despite her words. "They won't be happy if I open my doors to you."

I nodded. She was probably right.

"Why the subterfuge?" she asked. "I'm sure you have

plenty enough money to buy your own place and not feel a pinch in the pocket. Why rent mine?”

Honestly, I’d wondered the same thing.

“Nostalgia, I guess.” It was the closest thing to the truth I could offer her. “I have a lot of good memories here.” I’d been happy in the cottage with its pink curtains and cute kitchen.

Grace’s hand dropped from the door. “You can stay,” she finally said, though she didn’t invite me in. “I always thought there was more to the story than what you told Liam.” She reached out to touch my shoulder, and I felt like crying just from that small gesture of acceptance. “You were smitten with him, and you never seemed homesick while you were here. I figured you must have your reasons for ending things with him and staying away, but others aren’t so open-minded. They’ll take a while to come around. Assuming you’re not just here for a visit?” She arched a brow.

“I’m here to stay.” No amount of frostiness would deter me.

“Good.” She withdrew her hand. “Don’t make me regret my decision.”

“I won’t. I promise.”

Grace passed me a key from the pocket of her jeans. “Here. Let me know if you need anything.”

A fraction of the tension that had gripped me eased. “Thanks. Is there anywhere new I can buy dinner?”

“No.” She looked sympathetic. “The cafe will be closing at any moment. Other than that, it’s just the pub, unless you want to drive to the resort. Tabitha extended their coffee shop into a full restaurant a few years ago.”

Damn. No avoiding confrontation then.

“Okay.” I could do this. I needed to woman up and bite the bullet. There would be no driving to the resort, where I knew I’d get a warmer reception, just to avoid an uncomfortable situation that would have to happen sooner or later. It wouldn't be easy, but if it was a choice between temporary ease and long-term disappointment, there was no contest. "Thanks, Grace."

Next stop: Drunken Destiny.

LIAM

Is it possible to love and hate someone at the same time? - Unsent text message from Liam to Kennedy

The pub was relatively quiet. But then, it was a Monday night, and most of the locals were at home, so that was no surprise. I sat at a table near the bar, cradling a pint of beer and listening to Toby brag about the hot tourist from the resort he'd been hooking up with. Apparently she was Swiss, blonde, and adventurous as hell, although I tuned out most of his colorful description. The state of my own sex life was nonexistent, and I didn't need a reminder of how great his was. It would only make me feel pathetic.

I drank more beer. Thirty should be too young to feel this old. Toby was only five years my junior, and he was out there, playing the field. Why couldn't I bring myself to do the same anymore?

I reached for a chip and popped it into my mouth, scanning the other occupants of the pub while Toby rhapsodized about his hookup's killer body. Dad was behind the bar because it was Bailey's night off. Mum and a couple of her friends sat on stools, chatting to each other and bringing him into their conversation every now and then.

A group of weather-beaten men clustered in the back, alternating between drinking and playing darts. They were doing surprisingly well considering how much beer they'd drunk. But then, these craggy old guys could put booze away like no one's business.

"…you, Liam?"

"Huh?" I snapped around. Toby and Asher, my best friend, were looking at me, both wearing wry smiles.

"I asked if you've been seeing anyone lately," Toby said, apparently unconcerned that I'd zoned out.

I huffed. "No."

"That makes…."—Toby pretended to do math in his head—"a fucking long time without any action, am I right?"

Asher gave him a light shove. "Don't be an asshole. We can't all be as girl crazy as you. Some of us actually have to work around here."

Toby launched into a protest about how being a ski instructor counted as a real job, even if he was technically only employed for half the year. I sent Asher a smile, grateful for the distraction. He knew I hated anyone prying into my affairs. Especially when there wasn't anything to talk about.

I tuned back in to the conversation, and that was when the pub fell eerily silent. I looked around, expecting to see that someone had broken a plate or a chair, but nobody cursed or shouted an apology. Instead, all attention was focused on the door, where a woman stood silhouetted against the rapidly descending darkness.

Fuck. It couldn't be.

I stared, taking in the long blonde hair that was darker at the roots, the cute upturned nose, and the unique eyes I thought I'd never gaze into again for as long as I lived.

Kennedy.

She was back in Destiny Falls. In the pub. Only a handful of yards away.

Why was she here?

Someone coughed, breaking the hush. Eyes burned into me as our audience waited to see how I'd react so they could follow my lead. The community had been a great source of support when she first made a name for herself in Hollywood. They'd rallied around me, boycotting everything Kennedy Carter. The store had refused to sell any tabloids with her picture on the front. The movie theater had never played the films she starred in. And if anyone ever happened to learn anything about her, they sure never mentioned it to my face. A few had gone further and helped shield me from reporters who'd come to town, trying to dig up dirt about Kennedy's time in Destiny Falls. Now, she was here. Inexplicably.

I had no doubt someone here would toss her out if I gave any indication that was what I wanted. Hell, either Asher or Toby would gladly volunteer for the job. I just needed to force myself to move.

"Liam." Someone jostled my elbow. Firm fingers gripped it. "Let's go, man."

It was Asher, trying to get me to leave. But I couldn't look away from the woman who'd crushed my heart and stolen my future.

"What the fuck is she doing here?" he muttered. "Come on."

I stood up.

"Help me, Tobes," Asher urged.

Before my brother could move, Kennedy lifted her chin and crossed the room. I caught a waft of her scent as she stopped in front of me. Slightly sweet but unfamiliar. My throat threatened to close over. I didn't even know what she smelled like anymore. Somehow, that made me want to kick shit down.

I could still read her face though. She was nervous. Rightfully so.

Asher tugged my arm again. "Liam has nothing to say to you," he snapped at her.

It wasn't true. I'd had plenty to say to her over the years. Questions, angry rants, random observations I knew she'd have appreciated. But she hadn't been around to share them with. Because she hadn't wanted me enough to stay—or rather, to come back.

"Can we talk?" Her voice was deeper than it used to be. Smoother. That tiny discrepancy jolted me into action.

"I wanted to talk eleven years ago," I bit out, "but you weren't interested. So no, we can't talk." I brushed past her, heading for the exit with Toby and Asher flanking me. As soon as the door swung shut behind me, I released a shaky exhale. "Did that just happen?"

"Yeah, mate." Asher clapped me on the back. "Come on. We're going back to your place."

"She's in Destiny Falls." I could scarcely believe it. Kennedy had become something of an urban legend in these parts. The Hollywood It Girl who'd broken the hometown boy's heart—discussed in whispers behind my back but never, ever to my face. "Why the fuck is she here?"

"Who cares?" Asher guided me to my Ute. "I'm driving. Toby, you get beer and meet us there. We're going to need lots of it."

Toby saluted. "Aye aye, captain."

I climbed numbly into the passenger seat, registering that it felt odd not to be driving my own vehicle, but my whirring thoughts kept me from dwelling on it as Asher started the engine. Kennedy Carter—or Cox, whatever stage name she was calling herself these days—had a lot of nerve showing up in my father's pub.

"She won't stay," I murmured to myself. I needed to

remember that, and hold onto my anger at her for leaving without even giving me the chance to consider going with her. Many years had passed, but no matter what had brought her back here, I couldn't afford to let her into my life. Kennedy was a chapter of my past that needed to remain closed.

A Place to Belong

About the Author

Alexa Rivers writes about genuine characters living messy, imperfect lives and earning hard-won happily ever afters. Most of her books are set in small towns, and she lives in one of these herself. She shares a house with a neurotic dog and a husband who thinks he's hilarious. When she's not writing, Alexa enjoys travelling, baking cakes, eating said cakes, cuddling fluffy animals, drinking copious amounts of tea, and absorbing herself in fictional worlds.